THE SILENT MESSAGE

Morgan Rivers

CONTENTS

1. Chapter 1   1

2. Chapter 2   5

3. Chapter 3   10

4. Chapter 4   15

5. Chapter 5   21

6. Chapter 6   26

7. Chapter 7   31

8. Chapter 8   37

9. Chapter 9   42

10. Chapter 10   48

11. Chapter 11   53

12. Chapter 12   59

13. Chapter 13   65

14. Chapter 14   72

15. Epilogue   80

Chapter 1

Rain. I hate rain. Unfortunately, that is all it ever does here now. Since many of the world's governments agreed to spray the atmosphere with some chemical crap to make the greenhouse gasses dissipate, it has rained for the last four and a half months straight. They say it will pass, but at the moment I doubt it. The original estimate was just a month of rain, but we are well past that now. Some days it is little more than drizzle. Mostly though, it ranges from a light downpour to a heavy torrent.

It wouldn't be too bad, if the rain was safe. It isn't. Usually a moment or two in the rain is not bad, your clothes may sizzle a little. On some days, more than five minutes in the rain and you could end up with a minor burn or two. However, on heavy rain days if you spend more than twenty minutes outside they will definitely be picking up your charred corpse from the pavement.

My friend Samar thinks it is all part of a conspiracy instigated by 'The Feds', as he calls them. Allegedly, 'they' were all running out of money so 'they' caused all this dangerous rain so that 'they' can tax the heck out of umbrella and waterproof retailers, and other products aimed at helping you to keep dry or just safe from injury from the rain. I'd be inclined to believe him if the rain protection being sold actually worked longer than two or three outings.

Standing under the bus shelter waiting for my bus home, almost crowded out by too many under too small a space, I stared out at the puddles. It was a light downpour day. This morning I'd showered in BurnStop, a new product you can buy online, so the likelihood of injury was greatly reduced. It had probably worn off by now, I have no idea how long it should last, so there was no way I was standing in the rain.

An elderly gentleman stumbled along the street. He tripped a couple of times, his bare hand landing in a small puddle. You could hear the sizzle for each raindrop. He was disheveled, and there were holes burned in his clothes. The rain had been taking its toll; you could see sores developing through the holes.

He stood up and ran his hand through his scraggly, grey hair. Again, there a sizzle as the rain water ran over his scalp. I started to feel sorry for him, but I didn't want to leave the protection of the shelter. However, I couldn't stop looking his way.

The old guy stumbled again as he stepped forward, but he didn't fall this time. We locked eyes; I immediately regretted it. He had this worrying look of recognition. When he pointed my way my heart began to race. This was one of 'the burned', a new underclass of people who were unfortunate, homeless vagrants. They took shelter where they could, but were often moved on by the autocops. Robotic police have no emotions, they have no compunction about moving people out of their temporary shelters.

"Gor-," he spluttered, still pointing at me. He swallowed hard and blinked a few times. "Gordon Twist!" he yelled.

I wanted to die. Everyone else in the bus shelter just turned to me with complete terror on their faces. Even behind their masks, the wide, staring eyes told me I was the object of their fear. They parted like I was infected with a deadly disease. I, like everyone else, was wearing my re-breather. My last virus check proved I was clean, as did my green health band on my wrist. I was no threat to these people.

A burly woman to my left grabbed my arm and flung me out of the shelter. She was so quick I had no time to react. Now I was standing out in the rain in the middle of the road, with this weird old guy stumbling towards me.

"Hey! I don't know the guy!" I shouted. I pointed at the old guy in exasperation.

"I, we," she gestured to the others in the shelter, "don't care." They closed ranks, closer than before, and would not engage with me at all. I was trying to shove my way back into the shelter, but I was being pushed back every time. I stopped, raised my hands in defeat and backed off as I could see autocops beginning to converge on the shelter. That was a level of trouble everyone could do without.

The old guy reached me by then, and grabbed my arm. "Gordon, you need this," and he pushed a piece of paper into my hand.

"Look, I don't want anything from you," I said and I tried to return the note.

The old gasped, and fell to his knees. "No, take it. You will need it soon," he gurgled.

"Why?" I asked.

"Read the note. Find the truth," he said as he fell backwards.

I tried to catch him, but the conditions made it hard. His sodden clothing just slipped through my gloved hands.

"Go," he said. It was his last action. His stare became glassy and there was a sickening evacuation of air through his wrinkled lips.

I stared in horror as the commotion around me grew. I was frozen in time and it felt like hours were passing instead of minutes. I had time to watch everything in slow motion as various groups closed in around me and the dead man. Medics had turned up for Dead Guy, autocops were there taking IDs and statements from onlookers, and a real crowd was building.

The note in my hand brought me out of my stupor somewhat.

I unfurled the balled up paper. No, this was thicker. Older. More like parchment. In a practised hand there were written some names, of which mine was one. There were nine names I total, and mine was the only one not crossed out. There was also a single line of neatly underlined text that read:

Your safety is of utmost importance to us.

"Yeah, sure," I thought, "except there is someone that just died a few minutes ago!"

CHAPTER 2

I stood there staring at the note, unaware of the events and people around me. I was especially unaware of the autocop officer standing beside me.

"I am officer Z7@East", it repeated when I didn't respond. "Please supply your statement of truth." Autocops have no emotions, which helps when solving crimes, but I was sure this one was showing impatience. The voice was raspy and alien through the speaker grill in the centre of the autocops humanised face, and it sounded irritated.

I turned to look it squarely in the artificial, camera-based eyes that were above the speaker, the lenses were moving in and out as they tried to focus on me.

"Truth?" I scoffed a little. "I don't know him! He came over shouting my name but I've never seen him before. Ever. She," I pointed out the woman who'd pushed me out of the shelter, "threw me over here, where that guy then grabbed me and then he died. I tried to stop him falling but he slipped through my fingers. Wet gloves," I said as I held my hands up. The water glistened on them.

The autocop twitched it's head to one side, an affectation to make it seem more human, but I knew it was a prepro-grammed response. "Remove your gloves and then place your left hand here and repeat your statement," it said as it was showing me a TruthTaker, a dull grey box about the size of an ancient book. Every autocop carried one.

The TruthTaker was a sophisticated invention that reduced the elapsed time for criminal investigations. In shape it was based on what I've been told was a bible, a book for an old religion only a few people followed these days. It was really little more than the next level in what twentieth and early twenty first century folk would have called a lie detector. Only this device had built in consequences. It could detect lies with a very high success rate; there was less than a one percent failure rate. If this device caught you in a lie, it would administer a high voltage electric shock.

Tentatively I placed my hand, palm down, onto the sensor plate and repeated my claim. There were a few seconds of anxious waiting while the TruthTaker clicked and beeped. Finally the sensor plate lit up in a bright green and I let it a breath I didn't realise I'd been holding.

"Thank you Citizen Twist. Please go about your day," said the autocop.

I walked away as the medics and autocops about their business. There was a street cafe across the road and I could with some caffeine to settle my nerves.

As soon as I was in the vicinity of the entrance I felt the telltale rumble on my health band. The cafe's sensors were testing my health condition, which had been given a green status just week. The doors to the cafe opened as I approached as proof that I was safe to enter.

I shook off the good of my coat and saw a table near the counter was free. A waitress smiled at me and offered to take me over, I nodded and followed.

"Coffee, please," I said. "Black, hot."

"Certainly, sir," she said and scurried off.

Once I'd sat down, I pulled out my tablet and called Samar. I really need the advice of my oldest friend. We grew up in the same housing block, and despite his sometimes odd views he was really tuned in to what happened around the world.

It took a few rings for Samar to reply, but he eventually did. His face came into view on my screen and I realised why he'd taken his time to answer. His groggy, sleepy eyes stared inquisitively of the screen.

"This better be good, man. I've been on nights week," he slurred.

"I've just watched a man die in East Square," I said without preamble.

Samar was immediately awake. His face changed from sleepy to alert in a blink of his eyes. "Say that again, but this with details," he said.

My coffee turned up, and I took a big gulp of it before starting. I could see Samar moving about his obsessively new apartment making a cup of coffee for himself as I recounted what I saw.

"And the autocops let you go?" he asked.

"They had no reason to keep me," I said.

"But what about this note?"

"Here it is," and I showed it to the cam on my tablet. "I didn't tell them about it at all. Never even crossed my mind to be honest."

"Hey, hold it still and I'll scan it. Maybe there is something I can find on those names that are crossed out." Samar was amazing with computers and everything online so I was happy to let him have a go with whatever he was thinking. "That paper, if that is what it is, looks very old. Nice handwriting too."

I held the sheet as still as possible and waited for Samar to tell me he had a copy.

"Got it," he said.

I neatly folded the note and placed it my pocket. "Right, I'm off. I think another bus home will be here in a few minutes. Let me know what you find," I said. I then grabbed my coat and stuffed my arms hastily into the sleeves.

"No worries," Samar said whilst trying to stifle a yawn. I closed the call and headed for the exit.

As I was dashing out I placed my thumb on the pay sensor near the door, shouted my thanks and ran back out into the rain. I dropped my tablet back into my coat pocket and crossed the road over to the bus shelter.

I was the only one there, Dead Guy and the other travellers that had been here before were nowhere to be seen.

A moment later a bus pulled up and the doors hissed open. I stepped onboard, pressed my thumb to the fare-point, waited for the 'ting' my payment was successful and then walked to an empty seat.

The bus ride home was full, as usual, and I could feel myself nodding off. The adrenaline from the events at the bus shelter and the coffee were wearing off. Fatigue was really setting in. I forced my eyes to remain open long enough to get to my destination.

I stood near my stop and pressed the button to alert the driver. As the bus stopped I walked to the doors and exited. When the cold evening air hit me I was brought out of my sleepy state. A deep breath filled my lungs, I felt glad to be home.

CHAPTER 3

I sighed the heavy sigh of a long and tiring day as elevator carried me to my apartment on the twenty third floor. The garish light of the fluorescent bulb started to grate on me as it flickered and buzzed. The building manager, James Hech Esq., was barely interested in the basics. He was more inclined to berate residents for the smallest of misdemeanours. Coughing in the corridor even when wearing a mask or re-breather, being outside your apartment without a mask, or possibly a health band not being visible within the public spaces of the apartment block, small things. Things not against the law. The light in the elevator, or even the graffiti on the walls were ignored. As was the cleanliness of the public spaces.

When the doors opened on my floor, the the last thing I wanted to see was Hech. He was standing there with his mask in one hand and a half-chewed, pink nicotine stick in the other.

"Mr Twist," his smarmy voice made my skin crawl. The look-you-up-and-down eyes he always gave me made me shudder. He swallowed and took another bite of the nicotine stick and started to chew.

"Mr Hech. How are you?" I asked as I stepped past him.

"Fine. Fine. Just running my rounds," he smiled again. His breath stunk of the strawberry essence the nicotine stick had been flavoured with, but it was mixed with something stale. The stench was strong even through the filters on my re-breather and I struggled to hide my revulsion. Thankfully my mouth was covered so it was made easier.

Hech stepped in to the elevator. "You keep wearing that mask now," he said. I nodded. "Oh," he said and I turned around to face him. His tattooed left hand holding the doors of the elevator back. "Someone came round to see you earlier. An old guy. Told him you'd gone to work." He smiled that awful, knowing smile of his and then retreated in to depths of the elevator again.

I watched in horror as the doors closed. I stood there a moment longer as the floor display counted down to zero.

It took a force of will to make my feet move. Walking to my front door was a challenge. Thoughts of Dead Guy pointing at me dominated my thoughts so much that I barely recognised that my front door was ajar.

Before I properly touched the fingerprint lock the door swung gently away from me. There was no chance the lock mechanism had time to register my touch. I pushed the door wider and looked gingerly inside.

"Hello?" I called. There was a nervous wobble to my voice. No answer. Hech had done his 'rounds', so it was hard to believe he'd not seen this. "Hello," I called again. This time with more confidence, or at least I hoped. Still no response. I pulled out my tablet and called the emergency services.

A robotic voice responded. "Policing. What assistance do you require Citizen Twist?" There was no screen image, just an oscillating, animated line when the responder spoke.

"Someone has broken into my apartment, my stuff has been gone through and disturbed all around," I said as I looked about at my broken things and the clearly ransacked living room.

"Please stay still, and do not touch anything. An Auto Investigator officer has been dispatched. It will arrive in a moment," said the voice.

The call was disconnected and I stood there in stunned silence. A creeping dread came over me and I could not shake the feeling that Hech was involved. He must be; there is no way he didn't see the open door.

My phone app buzzed, and I was startled by the noise in the quiet of my turned-over living room. It was Samar.

"Hey, man. What did you find? Anything?" I said. I kept the camera focused on my face, hiding my living room.

"Where are you?" he said. No preamble as ever.

"Home?" I said.

"Not good. Get out of there. Soon as," he said.

My confused look was enough to prompt him to share his screen. "Does this guy look familiar?"

It was a photo of Dead Guy, sure he was a few years younger, but it was unmistakable. He was there with four other people. They were coming out of a large, municipal building. I didn't recognise the building. "Who is he?" I asked.

"No idea, but I reckon you know the man behind." Samar zoomed the image to the blond-haired man standing behind Dead Guy. It was my Dad. My Dad was smiling, obviously having shared a joke with Dead Guy and the other three in the photo. "I can name the other three on this pic," he said.

"Don't tell me-," I started, but Samar was not finished.

"Yes, their names are on the list you gave me." He returned the image back to his face, his eyebrows were raised high. "Come on, man. Go! Get here. Fast."

"I can't, I am waiting for the autocops. Someone has-" I began to say.

"Someone has turned your place over?" he asked.

"Yeah," I showed him round with the cam on my tablet.

"Crap. Not surprised. Okay. Play it cool with the autocops. Let them in, then get here," he said.

We ended the call just as the autocop knocked on my door.

"Citizen Twist, are you available," squawked the autocop at my door.

"Please enter," I replied.

The autocop hovered into my living room. "Please give me your statement of truth," it said as it proffered the TruthTaker.

I placed my hand on the sensor plate of a TruthTaker for what was not only the second time today, but the second time in my entire life. It disquieted me with the way my day, and my life, was going.

The autocop was motionless while I recounted the events of my day. I started with leaving for work, my dull day at ZenTech reviewing run logs and inspecting load manifests, I mentioned all the people I interacted with, the event at the bus shelter, and then my trip home. I mentioned meeting Hech and his claim of doing the rounds, his odd reference to Dead Guy and I finished with describing my apartment. I particularly left out the conversation with Samar; I felt that was not relevant to how my apartment looked right now.

"Thank you Citizen Twist. Do you have somewhere to stay for this evening while the investigation is conducted?" said the autocop.

"I do, I will call my friends," I said trying to sound casual about it.

The autocop nodded. "Your dwelling will be secured once the investigation is complete and a full report will be submitted with any findings detailed. You will also receive a copy of that report," it said. "You may return to your dwelling once you receive the report."

I nodded and left as soon as I could. However, I waited until I was in the elevator before calling Samar.

"Yo, on my way," I said as soon as I saw his face on screen.

"Cool. Stay safe but get here quick. Don't tell anyone," he said. "You didn't tell the autocops did you?"

I shook my head, "Ten minutes," I said and we ended the call.

CHAPTER 4

The ten minute walk over to Samar's was stressful. I kept running the images of Dead Guy falling down in front of me and not being able to catch him. Thankfully, the rain had settled down to a light drizzle so the walk itself was not unpleasant. I just could not shake the feeling that I was in danger.

I kept looking over my shoulder as I walked. Paranoia was beginning to set in. A road sweeper bot shuffled along toward me and at first I thought it was heading straight for me, it's single beady, red eye looked ominous and determined, but it was only trying to get some litter I'd not spotted. It stopped and allowed me to walk by before picking up the discarded rubbish. The red-eye camera of the sweeper bot then began searching about again looking for more litter. I moved away swiftly.

Samar's housing block was just across the street, I was almost safe. Just the road to cross. It was prudent to use the crossings or risk the wrath of the autocops, but I wanted to get there sooner rather than later. I stepped one foot onto the road and immediately regretted it. A small van came hurtling by and almost took me with it in the backdraft. I retreated and headed further down the road to find a crossing.

The words from the note came back to the front of my brain, "Your safety is the utmost importance to us." Who wanted me safe though, I just could not work out why I was on someone's list.

My mind went to the picture Samar showed me. It was definitely my Dad in the photo and Dead Guy. I hoped I was wrong, but one thing that I recall about it was they all seemed to be wearing the same clothing. Maybe a uniform? I would have to look at the picture again to be sure.

I managed to reach the front doors of Samar's block; the sensors on the entry way scanned me and my health band and I was allowed to enter. I was not able to go too far in as I would need to contact a resident to allow me to enter the inner door. I pinged the console next to the inner door and punched in the apartment number for Samar.

"Hey Samar, it's me. Can you open up?" I said. There was a buzz and the door opened so I entered and headed for the elevator.

We used to live in the same block, but when my mother died I was unable to keep the apartment. My salary was not enough for this building, so I had to find another place to live. Hech's building was the cheapest and nearest one I found. Samar was luckier though. He still lived in the apartment he grew up in and his parents funded the apartment for him to keep while they lived in retirement luxury in another country. Spain, I believe. The whole building was a completely different experience to mine. We lived close, but it may as well be different planets. This building was clean and tidy and smelled fresh. The elevator even played music while it rose to Samar's floor. A light ding played as we reached his floor and the doors smoothly opened. I smiled at the whole experience and was mildly pleased not to see Hech's punchable face looking at me.

I walked to Samar's door and rapped on it. Inside I could hear Samar bound over to the door and unlock it. The door swung briskly inward and Samar's bright face greeted me.

"Gordon, great! You made it in one piece," he said.

"One piece?" I asked.

"Yeah, was worried for a moment. You told no one, right?"

I shook my head.

"Excellent. Now, this image. I've done more digging," he said and ushered me into his apartment.

I wandered to the living room and saw three monitors connected up to his computer. He worked from home, agoraphobia he called it, I just think he liked staying out of the rain as much as possible. In another corner of the room was an exercise treadmill, one of those interconnected ones with a screen on it and whole load of sensors on to track whoever was using it at the time.

"You ever use that?" I said point to the treadmill and then at the pizza boxes piled high next to it.

"Course," he said. "Sometimes," he continued sheepishly.

We both laughed. I could not see Samar doing exercise. At school he always had a note or something to get him out of all sporting or otherwise physical events. He did the bare minimum.

"So, what did you find on this photo?" I asked.

He walked over to his desk and pulled up a chair for each of us. When he'd sat down he grabbed two beers from a cool box next to his chair and gave me one of them. I needed this and eagerly twisted off the lid and took a large gulp. It was cold and tasty.

Samar pressed a few keys and the image came back on screen. The image showed five men, two we knew - my Dad and Dead Guy. My fears earlier were confirmed, they were all wearing a uniform. It was a dark camouflage pattern suggesting military. That in itself placed the image to be around twenty years old. Along with the advances in technology, there has been a world-wide treaty, fragile as it may be, that military units be disbanded. We still have security forces, but these are largely automated and staffed by a minimum human contingent. The Oversight Committee. Other countries have similar.

"When was the last time you saw your Dad?" Samar asked.

"I would have been around ten years old," I said. "He died in that crash in '22. There were no survivors from the plane." I slumped in the seat as I remembered how hard it hit my mother when he died.

"Yeah, that was bad. I remember now, you didn't come to school for a whole month."

"He was going on a 'business trip', he said, and he would be back in a week. He gave me and my Mum a great big hug. I asked him for a present, and he said he would see what he could do. He never made it, though. I guess the business trip was a ruse given the uniforms," I said.

"Yes. I think you are right," Samar said. "This building does not exist. At least when I try to search for it, I find nothing. Given the style, I think it would have been early twentieth century, so there would likely be pictures every of it. An old building like that. But I can't find it anywhere. It doesn't even look like it was on a restricted base or anything, there is nothing around to indicate it was secured or anything like that."

He pointed out all these details and I just stared at my Dad the whole time. He looked younger than I remember, but memory is a tricky thing and he could easily pass for the same age as when he set off on that trip.

"Can I see the note?" Samar asked.

I fished it out of my pocket and handed it over. Samar smoothed it out and put it into his scanner. A moment later and the note was on his screen. He ran it through a few scans to see if he could clean it up; the paper it was written on was old and yellow. The creases in the paper, I had balled it up at one point, were not helping either.

He ran it through one more time at the highest resolution and seemed happier with the result. "So, lets see if we can do anything with this handwriting," he said.

"What do you mean?" I asked.

"Graphology. It's nonsense really, but sixteenth or possibly fifteenth century scholars," Samar added air quotes to 'scholars', "used to study hand writing and claimed it could lead to an inner understanding of the writer. Pseudoscience, but sometimes there may be something there to see," he smiled.

Samar zoomed in the image to get a closer look at the word 'Your', and then gasped.

"What?" I said.

"Look at that! Would you believe it? There is a hidden text on the paper," he said. He grabbed the paper off the scanner and held it up to a bright light.

The text was small, and faint, almost translucent in the paper. There was a series of numbers, separated in an ordered fashion and below that were four lines of text. The words were small and required the paper to be moved about to place them under the glare of the bright light, but the message was clear:

Protect Gordon. He is key to our continued survival.He must be allowed to grow to age.He cannot know until he is ready.

CHaPTer 5

I sat there in stunned silence. In all the things that can happen in my life, what does this mean?

"When will I be ready? What do I need to be ready for? Who needs to protect me? Why do I need protection? And will someone please, please, tell me what the hell is going on," I said. My voice increased in volume with each question. Anger was beginning to take hold.

"Hey, man, take a breath. I'm here, we will figure this out," said Samar.

His smiling face could not hide his concern. He was definitely worried about this. Samar has been known to harbour the odd conspiracy theory, and even voiced one to two, but I was never certain he really, deep down, believed in them. I saw the theories he espoused as a cry for attention. We didn't have many friends as kids, but we always had each other.

He and I were 'geeks', in the old terminology. A name that resurfaced during our teenage years. In the past geeks were socially shunned, but it became a badge of honour of sorts at one point, and was a popular moniker for many years in the early half of the twenty first century, but it has waned again since.

I stood, stormed over to the large window and took a few deep breaths. I looked out over the night time scene of the city and that helped me to centre myself.

The twinkling fairy lights on a window across the road in another housing block caught my eye and I stared at them a moment or two. "I just want answers," I said to the window. To the world. "Yesterday, heck, even this morning, everything was 'normal'. It was sane. The world has become strange and insane now."

"I get you, but we will get answers. Let it be for now and order some pizza-" Samar said.

I turned to Samar. "More pizza?" I said with a smirk on my face as I patted my belly.

"Yes, some pizza," Samar smiled. "With a beer or three and a holo-movie, maybe a classic, to take your mind off it all. You can have the bed in spare room when you want to sleep. Today has been long and traumatic. Tomorrow will look better, I promise," he said.

Samar ordered pizza, I clicked through the films on offer on Flix+.

"That one!" Samar screamed and pointed. "That's a classic." He laughed.

I didn't recognise the film, but then I'm not a film sort of guy. Samar was a complete film-nut, he even had a few posters from old movies, all recreations, decorating his walls. I didn't watch movies, so I didn't recognise any of them.

I tended to use holo-booths for my entertainment. Fighting dragons of myth or flying through the air in experimental shuttle planes. Sitting here with Samar though was a pleasant change. Even though I wasn't really watching the movie, I was enjoying the company.

There was a chime at the door ten minutes into the movie; pizza had arrived.

Samar returned with two pizza boxes and threw one into my lap. "Eat up," he said.

He flopped into his chair, pulled out a slice and took a bite. "You can't beat a piping hot slice," he said through a mouthful.

I took a bite of a slice of mine and immediately knew what he meant. We both laughed as a string of cheese dropped down my chin.

"Hey, I have been thinking," Samar said. "What if this was all part of some elaborate hoax?"

"Hoax? You mean that guy didn't really die in front of me?" I spat a lump of cheese as I spoke.

"No, nononono. I mean, what if this is all a big misunderstanding and then others have taken the baton up and just run with it," he said.

"I don't get it," I said. "You're Samar. King of the Conspiracy Theory. In fact multiple theories at one point if I remember correctly. And you're not curious?" I laughed.

Samar laughed back, but I saw something in his face.

"What?" I said.

Samar tried to change subject, "Nothing, man. Let's just watch the movie" His face started to flush, and I knew there was something.

"Pause movie!" I commanded, and the holo projector froze the playback. The shocked face of a young child staring at a mythical creature bowing to her friend glowed against the far wall.

"Hey, I was watching that," Samar said.

"Come on. Spill," I said.

Samar sighed and closed his pizza box. "Movie off," he said with resignation. "OK. You're right. There is a theory rattling around up here," and he tapped his temple. "But it's not fully formed yet."

"Just cut to it then," I said.

Samar took a swig of his beer, and then another. I just raised my eyebrows at him. He sighed again, and then began.

"It's all on your Dad. That picture is off. Way off. I tried to find when it was taken, but there was no time stamp in it. Nothing. It's clean. Like it has been scrubbed, or taken before digital photography," he said. He left that thought hanging in the air.

He took a moment or two, and Samar was waving his hands in a circular, trying to urge me on in my thinking.

Then it hit me, "Digital photography has been around for over one hundred years," I said. A scary thought was forming in my mind.

"It has," said Samar.

"But if that is the case-" I started.

"Yes?"

"If that is the case then that means-" the thought in my head was not really fully formed either.

"If that is the case, then this image was taken in the twentieth century," said Samar.

"Can we corroborate that theory at all?" I asked.

"The building. If we can find that building anywhere in the world then we can verify when it was built. If we can't then either it's a movie set, or it's a hidden location and our theory is all hogwash," Samar said.

CHapter 6

I waved away this silly notion that Samar had put forward. What nonsense. "Are you joking? Are you trying to say my Dad is-"

"Possibly a couple of centuries old. Yes, that is exactly what I'm saying," said Samar.

"Too many movies," I laughed. "And too many conspiracies. You need to go outside of your apartment sometimes too. Even if you just went downstairs to the communal area that would be better than being in here all day long," I said trying to sound kind.

"I go out," he said, feigning hurt feelings with a pouty face. "Sometimes," he laughed.

We both laughed, this was exactly what I needed tonight after the weird event this afternoon.

The graying face of Dead Guy as he breathed his last is something I'll never be able to forget. His finger pointing at me, willing me too help him, to maybe save him. I shuddered at the thought and looked over to my only friend.

Samar had started to nod off to sleep, a beer bottle drooping dangerously in his hand; threatening to spill the liquid within. I sprang to my feet and caught the bottle just before it fell. Samar didn't even notice. In those few seconds he'd fallen into a deep, drunken sleep. There was a blanket draped over the back of his chair, which I gently teased out from under him and then covered him with.

I am back to my chair and slumped into it. The holo projector was still on, despite the fact we'd stopped the movie itself a while ago. "Holo off," I said as quietly but firmly as I could. Samar snored in response.

My tablet in my bag was chirping, this would be the police calling to report on my apartment. "Okay, okay," I said at the insistent noise. After fishing out the tablet, I stared at it contemplating whether I should answer or not.

It took me a moment of staring to realise the caller was not the police. The caller's number was withheld in fact. Caller anonymity was outlawed, mainly to prevent spurious cold-calling or prank calling. I had always thought that all devices were set to provide caller details when you made a call, and you could not turn it off.

The green check mark, for answering calls, and the red cross, for reject, both wiggled and danced to each chirp. "Stuff it," I said, mostly to myself, and I hit the check mark.

"Hello," I said.

"Gordon, is that you? Your vid is off," said an unfamiliar female voice. The irony did not escape me; she hadn't turned on video either.

"Yes, vid is off. On purpose. Just like you. Who is this?" I asked.

The screen went from a dark green with a faceless head-and-shoulders icon to the face of my mother.

"Mum? But you're-" I started.

"Gordon, there's no time for this. I don't have long. Run. Run as fast as you can. Ditch any tech. But write down this number," she said.

She showed a scrap of paper with a hand written number on it. I scrabbled for a pen from my bag and wrote the number onto my palm.

"What is going on?" I asked as I wrote.

"Not on here. Find an old phone, there's one in the Museum of Tech downtown. It still works, just dial," and she ended the call.

I couldn't put the tablet down. My mind raced. It had been three years since my mother had died, but there she was on screen. As large as life. Larger. It was surreal this feeling of anger and elation running through me. If she wasn't dead, why had it taken so long for her to get in touch.

Then the thought hit me, who was in the coffin at her funeral?

"You gonna eat that or hug it?" Samar said.

"Huh?" was all I could manage.

"Your tablet, you're staring at it like it's a juicy steak or something," he said. "If you're that hungry have some more of your pizza." He laughed a little.

"I was going to call the police," I stuttered, "to get an update on my apartment." My voice cracking as I spoke, so I cleared my throat.

"Leave it to the morning, man. They may be robots but you're not. I'm off to bed. You can have the spare room," said Samar as he left to room. He was rubbing and stretching his neck as he left.

"Yeah, you're right. They'll probably call me anyhow," I said.

I then went to the spare room and hunted out a piece of paper. There were none in the room, so I went back to the living room and tore a chunk off one of the pizza boxes. Back in the spare room I carefully chopped the number from my palm.

Samar rattled about for a few minutes, getting ready for bed, and I waited for the best time. While I waited I turned off my tablet and put it back into my bag. My mother had said to ditch it, but I could do that. This was literally all I really had.

Back at the apartment was all my clothes and my furniture, obviously, but my tablet was everything else. Without that I had nothing.

After around an hour I crept out of the room and checked the living room. Samar was nowhere to be seen. I listened at his bedroom door and over light, easy-listening music I could hear deep breathing and the odd snore trekking me that Samar was asleep.

I picked up another pizza box and wrote a quick message to my friend.

Samar, my friend. Got to rush. I'll be in touch soon. Thanks for the pizza and the beers. You're amazing as ever. G.

I then quietly left.

CHAPTER 7

The elevator down was taking a long time, at least that is the way it felt. Maybe that was guilt for leaving Samar in the dark about what I was doing and where I was going. When the doors opened on the ground floor I hesitated about leaving and nearly pressed the up button again.

An elderly man in the lobby was just looking at me with expectant eyes. That was all I could see of his face, his rebreather was huge.

I shrugged and left and the old man entered the elevator. He was muttering something as he entered the elevator, but I let it slide. I'm not a person that seeks out conflict.

Before I opened the front door of Samar's building I could see the rain had built to a torrent. I didn't want to go outside. My coat would keep me safe for a few more trips in the rain, but who wants to go out in that? It wouldn't be long before sores would start to show.

Instead I pulled out my tablet and dialed for a taxi. An automated system led me through to a robotic dispatcher. It was an old model, probably no more than a head and shoulders; it wasn't going anywhere anyhow. The dispatcher was made to look like a dark haired woman, with a rubberised skin covering the robot within. It looked quite scary.

"Thannnk you for calling C4BCentral," stuttered the clunky, stilted voice. The speech module on the dispatcher was obviously an old one, or broken. Some of the syllables glitched with a gentle buzzing or were elongated . "What is your ... dezzztination?"

I thought the screen had frozen for a second, and then the dispatcher's mouth lit up in a creepy, artificial smile.

"I need to get to the Museum of Tech, downtown," I said.

The smile was replaced with a frown and a head tilt, to imitate the human trait when we think. "That will ... will ... will be 42 credits. Please pressss the fingerprint sen ... sensor."

I touched the sensor with my thumb, there was a light ding a second later.

"Thank you. A taxi will beeee there in zzeven minutes."

The dispatcher then ended the call and the image was replaced with a reference code that I would need to provide to be able to board when my taxi arrived.

I doubted the accuracy of the dispatcher, but I needn't have. In less than the time predicted I saw a track taxi with the C4BCentral livery pull up outside, and then there was a ping on my tablet. I pulled up my hood and headed outside.

The taxi was driverless, and the doors were locked as expected. There was a keypad next to the door handle where I tapped in the code I was sent and the door slid open. Once

I'd stepped inside the door closed, almost without letting me actually get on board. The taxi shot off and I thrown into the seat.

The drive to the museum was short, but when so when I got there the museum was shut. That was unexpected. Yes, it was late, but the museum never shuts. At least so I thought.

I got out of the taxi and headed for the big double doors at the entrance to the museum. There were no lights visible inside either. I was beginning to think I'd been led on a merry dance at the amusement of some unseen operator.

The doors were definitely locked when I tried them and I was about to turn around when I heard the taxi leave. Well, I was here now and the rain was unrelenting, so it was time to see if there was another way in.

I stepped back and assessed the best way to tackle this, and without actually thinking about it I chose to go left.

The rain just kept beating down, and I was about to give up when I saw a side door creak open. No one was around, no lights beyond the door, but I was getting wet. And this rain was not stopping. There didn't appear to be another choice.

"Hello?" I called into the darkness.

No answer.

"OK, please don't kill me," I said, mostly to myself, but hopefully to the person who'd opened the door. I then stepped inside.

Lights down the corridor flickered and buzzed into life as they sensed motion from me entering. I closed the door behind me and then headed towards the far end of the corridor. As I walked more lights ahead of me illuminated, and those

I'd left behind turned off. The corridor was not that long; despite the darkened lights behind me I could still see the door by which I'd entered. Eventually, the corridor came to an end at a set of doors labelled 'Storage and Archive'.

I took a deep breath and pulled the doors open. Beyond was a cavernous warehouse filled floor to ceiling with stacks and stacks of old technology. Many the items were covered in a thick layer of dust. Others had a clear plastic cover, which was also covered in a similar about of dust.

There was still no sign of life. ”Anyone here?” I called. ”Come on! This is getting silly,” I shouted.

Still no response.

I would have expected my coffee to echo in such a large room, but noises were disturbingly muffled by the sheer volume of stuff old crappy computers, strange, archaic movie displays, and all manner of things I could not identify. There was a collection of dust encrusted boxes labelled 'game consoles', which appeared to be categorised by year, or more accurately, generation of the technology itself.

Another stack I passed claimed to be 'telepones', and the standard icon I'd come to take for granted when making and trading calls on my tablet suddenly made sense. I lifted a an old red phone, with a set of numbers from zero to nine all laid out in a circle. It made no sense to me how this would have worked. There wasn't even a screen.

A noise from over to my right startled me and I neatly dropped the antique in my hands.

”Is someone there?” I said as I gently returned the dust covered telephone to its shelf.

I brushed my hands together to rid myself of dust and headed for the sound I heard. "Please, stop playing games. You asked me to come here, so here I am." Frustration laced my tone.

Ahead I heard a door closing, and I picked up my pace. Someone had just exited through another door to this archive, and I was intent on finding them.

I burst through the only door I could find, whoever it was must have gone this way. Another door up this corridor opened and then closed, so I sprinted over to where I'd heard the noise.

I pulled open the door and saw the main floor of the museum. This area was well lit, all the lights were on and so were any of the items on display.

"Gordon, I am glad you could make it," a voice from the mezzanine level above said.

I spun around to find who had spoken, nearly knocking over a nearby exhibit. Eventually my eyes locked onto those of my mother.

Standing next to her was my father, and both were smiling warmly at me.

"Dad? Mum? How are-" I stumbled over my words but I could not finish the sentence.

"Yes, son," said my father, "you're not seeing things. It is us."

"We have a lot to discuss, and there is more to do," said my mother.

"What do you mean?" I asked.

"There will be time for questions soon," said my father. "First though, it is time to leave here," he continued. He then gestured to someone I'd not seen who came quickly from my left, grabbed me and then injected me with something.

I recall the hissing sound of the hydrospray, and then nothing. Darkness claimed me.

CHAPTER 8

W hen I opened my eyes, it was too dark to see anything. I wasn't even sure I'd opened them, so I tried
blinking a lot just to test my eyelids. I could feel them moving;
there was no light in this room. No windows, no doors.
Nothing.

I came to realise I was laying on on a hard surface. There
was no comfort afforded at all. It felt like a metal slab, or a
table. I rapped my knuckles against it and there was a dull,
hollow ring. This was definitely not a table, and certainly
hollow. Feeling around I found the edge, and then the sides.
This was not a table, I would not find an underside. The
surface of what I lay upon smoothly met both sides, which
appeared to run to the floor.

My head felt groggy, and then the memory of being
drugged hit me. I tried to sit up, and the world lurched. Even
with no visual reference in this pressing darkness, I felt the
room spin.

I waited for a moment, half sitting up, half laying down. My head began to clear, and slowly I continued to sit up.

The darkness was scary, I had to control my breathing to prevent me having a panic attack. I felt around the walls trying to find the limits of my imprisonment. My hands were pressed against the smooth wall as I moved to my right and my hands brushed a light switch. The flare of the lights was almost blinding.

I squinted into the brightness to see I was in a small room, probably five feet by six. In the centre of the room was what could only be described as a plastic altar. It wasn't a bed, or a hospital gurney. It was smooth on all surfaces. There was a long mirror in one wall that I assumed was actually a one-way window like I've seen in holo movies.

Shading my eyes from the light I tried to peer through the glass, but I could only see myself reflected. Stepping back I noticed the door behind me also reflected.

I tried the door, but it was locked. I banged on the door again and again. "Hello! Is there anyone there!" I screamed. There was no response. I slammed my fists against the door again.

With no response, I started to panic. Thoughts raced through my head of where I was and who knew. No one knew; I'd not even told Samar. My only friend didn't know, and he was probably still asleep.

Thoughts of Samar made me think of how long is been here. It was night time when I arrived at the museum, but then I was drugged. How long was I asleep? Where even was this room? Was I even still at the museum?

Rage began to brew and I flew at the mirrored glass once again. "Who the hell are you people? What do you want with me?" I shouted at my reflection.

And then I laughed.

The venomous look I was throwing at whomever was behind the glass was actually quite comical. I'm not an angry person. Every one I know will tell you I'm quite timid. Samar hates how I have never pushed myself forward.

I slumped against the altar and started to fish through my pockets for something to distract me.

"You know," I said to the emptiness around me, "I'm not normally like this. All angry and all that. I hate arguing, violence and confrontation. You've really caught me on a bad day." I chuckled to myself.

"I don't know who you are, or what you want, but it would be nice to actually speak to someone," I said. My neck ached where is been injected. "It would be nice if you could tell me what you put in my neck too." I rubbed my neck too try and ease the pain.

"Where am I? Is this a part of the museum?" I asked.

There was no response; I hadn't expected one to be honest. There was probably no one being the glass either, but I carried on.

"What do you want?" I said very loudly. I wasn't shouting, I'd done enough of that. This was just a raised voice, an increase in volume. I was totally calm, or at least I wanted anyone watching to believe that at least.

There was a crackle, followed by a his, on a speaker above the mirrored glass that I'd not noticed before. It was as white at the walls around it, no wonder I missed it.

"Gordon, it's me," it was my Mum's voice, "sweetheart listen, the people I work for need something from you. Then they'll let you go free."

"Yeah right," I said. I stood up suddenly and marched over to the glass. "People who want help don't kidnap someone they want help from."

"I know it's hard to understand, but it's true," she replied.

"Hard to understand? Are you on something?" I said.

"Gordy, I-" she started.

"Don't call me that," I said. "You lost that privilege when you left. The autocops said you'd been killed, said they had a body. They said you'd been killed in a violent attack. We even had a funeral, Samar was the only person there other than me, but we had one. Your 'body' was in a beautiful white coffin," my voice started to break as emotions threatened to overwhelm me. "I guess that the person we cremated was-"

"It was a homeless person we found dead from hyperthermia that looked like me," interrupted my mother.

"So you dressed her like you, and then you what? You disappeared?" Confusion and emotion fought for control of my temper.

"It was the only choice. It was that or they would come for you and take what they wanted. They wouldn't have cared if you lived or died. With me out of the way, you entered the social care system, and with that came a level of protection," she said.

"You're making no sense!" I said and I kicked the door. "How does you disappearing make me safe?"

"Gordon, I know it's hard, but I was doing what I thought was best. I was under a lot of pressure," she said.

"I was seventeen. I still needed my Mum," I started to cry. Tears were running down my face as my emotions got the better of me.

CHAPTER 9

I sat slumped up against the door, crying. Tears streamed down my face and I couldn't stop them. My mother had eventually stopped taking to me when I'd stopped responding.

There was no point talking to anyone. I'd been tricked into coming here. Tricked into believing that I would get answers to this mystery. No one wanted to give me answers, at least none that made sense.

She would not tell me who was behind this scheme. However, she insisted that I was only safe if those after me thought my parents were dead.

I just sat there in silence, not even moving. Time passed. I had no idea how long, and I started to notice the buzzing of the fluorescent light above. Squinting, I tried to focus on the cause. The light itself seemed to get brighter and brighter until I had to shut my eyes.

When I opened them again, I was outside. Before me was the door to Samar's building and I had a sudden thought that I'd dreamt being at the museum. I wanted to check the time, but my bag was missing. My tablet, and everything I had within the bag were gone.

In a panic, I looked about. My bag was no where to be seen. It was then I realised there was no rain, I wasn't even wearing a raincoat.

The screen of the call panel on the door of the building was flickering. I was drawn to it; there was an urge to call for Samar. I went to press the buttons for his apartment, but the screen glitched.

It was taking a few seconds for the glitch to clear, and there was a buzzing again. I scrunched my eyes until I saw stars then I reopened them to more confusion.

The touch screen based panel had been replaced with an old fashioned button key panel. There was no screen, just the numbers zero to nine, the hash symbol and an asterisk. Above the numbers was a circular speaker grill.

There was no one around. I looked up and down the street, but not even vehicles were around. I would have thought that there should have been at least a bus, or a taxi, or something. At all hours of the day and night, traffic still flows.

I turned back to the call panel and was greeted with the familiar call panel with a touch screen. An ad for BurnStop was playing on screen. Tapping the screen stopped the ad and the image was replaced with a set of numbers as I was used to seeing.

Cautiously, I typed in Samar's apartment number and waited. The image to the right of the keys usually shouted an image of the owner. This time though, no image appeared. Just a generic head-and-shoulders silhouette.

"Hello?" said a woman's voice. There was no video.

"Who's this?" I said.

"What the hell? You called me!" she replied and then promptly hung up.

Confused I tried again. The call tone rang three times, and the woman returned. "Look if you don't leave me alone I'll call the police," she said.

"I'm looking for someone," I blurted out. "My friend Samar."

"Samar? You mean my three month old baby boy? How can you be his friend? Weirdo! Leave now or I call the cops." There was a sharp buzzing noise, and the line went dead.

What was going on? Samar is a baby? I tried the number for my old apartment. When I was a child my family and I lived in this block too, so in theory someone I know should answer.

The call tone was different to what I remembered. It rang twice, and then was answered. "Gordon, you need to run." It was my mother again.

"Run? But I-" I started to say.

"Gordon, you need to run," she repeated.

"Where am I to go?" I shouted.

"Gordon, you need to run," she said a third time.

I saw a car pull up a few feet away. The windows were darkened so I couldn't see who was inside. The back doors on both sides opened and out stepped two men in grey suits. The both looked at me and stared.

The speaker to my right was vying for my attention. "Gordon, you need to run!"

Now I understood, and I bolted down the street.

A glance over my shoulder showed the men in grey running behind me, each of them drawing a concealed weapon; a foot long staff, which glowed with a blue-black light that I couldn't look at properly. The stoic faces of the men in grey, despite the effort of running, told me that they would have no compunction about causing me harm.

I ducked down an alley to the right, but I could could still hear my mother's voice. "Gordon, you need to run."

"I am running!" I screamed at the surrounding walls.

The alley turned left ahead, right into a chain link fence. A gate in the centre was padlocked shut. I could hear the pounding feet of the men behind me, I needed to get out of here. Up was the only way to go.

I clawed at the fence and began my ascent. There was a barbed wire running along the top, when I was neat the top my hand gripped right onto a barb. It bit deep onto my palm. I could not stop though.

The men in grey turned the corner just as I was straddling my leg over the fence. I was careful to avoid the barbs. I grinned at them both and started to move my other leg over the fence.

Ominously, they just grinned back. The tallest of the two men stepped calmly over to the fence and touched the blue-black end of his staff to the fence.

Time felt as though it slowed. I saw a blue spark pass from the staff, onto the fence and then multiply to travel in all available directions. The shock of electricity passed through each link in the fence and then into each pole. The padlock on the gate fizzed and popped, and then quietly exploded. The spark of power ran up to the barbed wire, and then into me.

I was frozen in place. Paralysed by fear and electric shock, I saw the other man in grey reach for something in his pocket. It looked like an old phone. He placed it to his ear and spoke. I could see his lips move, but could not hear what he was saying.

The world around me began to get bright again. Too bright, as if I was still staring at the fluorescent tube light in the white room back in the museum.

I had to close my eyes again. The intensity was burning. My eyes felt like they could explode and there was a smell of cooking flesh.

Something was pushing against my back, but I still could not open my eyes. The pushing sensation grew in pressure until eventually I felt myself falling.

No, not falling. Sliding. Being pushed along the smooth floor by the door.

I opened my eyes and I was in the white room again. Or possibly still. I can't possibly have left here. The memory of being chased was starting to fade. Was that a dream? A nightmare? Or really a memory. I could not keep my eyes open any longer and had to shut them again.

"Get him back into the conditioning room," I heard a male voice say. I didn't recognise the voice.

I was unable to open my eyes, it hurt to try. In my head I could hear me screaming, shouting. 'Let me go,' I was saying, but no one heard me. My lips were as frozen as the rest of me.

"Do we really need him alive?" said another voice. A female voice, but not my mother's.

"Of course we do," said a third voice. This one, a male, I did recognise.

CHAPTER 10

Through sheer emotion, I forced myself to open my eyes. The light was still too bright, I had to squint. Even so, I looked right into the eyes of my oldest friend. I immediately felt betrayed.

"Samar?" I said. My voice trembled and cracked. It was like I'd not spoken in a while, my throat felt dry and scratchy.

The man with the face of my friend laughed haughtily. "Ha! My name's not Samar," he spat. I had known Samar my entire life, our parents were friends first, and it made sense that so were we. We spent a lot of time with each other over the years.

Obviously in charge here, the person I thought I knew then turned to his colleagues, "Get him fastened down!"

It was then I realised I was being strapped onto a gurney. I was unable to move my ankles, they were held fast by the man I didn't recognise. The woman was getting frustrated trying to fasten a strap over my left wrist. Not-Samar, I had no other name for him, was holding my head in place.

I swung my free arm up and knocked the woman backwards. Not-Samar went to catch her and that left my head free. I reached over to my left and stared to undo the strap. At the same time I kicked out at the man holding my ankles. My heel connected with his face. He fell to his knees, blood streaming from his ruined nose.

By the time Not-Samar had picked up the woman, I'd freed my hand. I looked about and saw I was no longer in the white room, this appeared to be a long corridor. Ahead I could see an old fashioned exit sign, lit up in green. That was where I needed to go.

"Gordon," said Not-Samar, "come on now 'old friend'." The emphasis on 'old friend' made me cringe. He stood there with his hands out, his eyes darted to the man in the floor clutching his face, and whimpering.

The woman was looking at the man with the broken nose, but he waved her away. I looked for a way to defend myself and saw a mop standing in its bucket a couple of feet behind me. Keeping my eyes on Samar and the woman, I started to walk backwards to the mop.

"Don't be stupid now," said the woman as she stood and took a step towards me. She obviously saw what I was trying to do.

They were trying to get around me, surround me. I smirked. My foot then kicked the mop bucket, a tell-tale scrape of metal against a tiled floor. I reached behind and grasped the mop handle. With a quick swing, I brought the mop in front. The arc of my swing flung dirty water over both Not-Samar and the woman.

They both flinched at the water and I took that as my cue. I rushed forward, the mop held horizontally. I hit both Not-Samar and the woman with one end each. Samar got the mop head.

The handle snapped and I barrelled on through. Charging for the exit sign. The sign told me the way out was to my right, and I carried on running for the door.

I pushed the bar in the centre of the door and it moved easily away from me. The scene outside was unlike anything I expected.

It was sunny, there were some birds being fed a few feet away by a woman who looked like she'd not changed her clothes in days. The road was filled with old style cars not seen since the early twenty first century. People were everywhere, and no one was wearing a raincoat. It was warm, and no clouds were in the sky at all.

It was a bewildering sight.

The confusion was enough to stall me. Not-Samar had recovered, and he brought help. Two large hands gripped me tight around both of my biceps. I struggled and wriggled and knew almost immediately it would be hard to break free from these giant hands.

"Come on now, Gordon," said Not-Samar. His voice was soft and calming, his face showed no emotions.

"Help me!" I shouted, screamed, to a group of people passing by. No one looked.

"These people won't help you. They have their own lives to deal with," he said. His voice remained on the same level. The brute behind me didn't speak.

I still had half of the broken mop handle in my hand, I looked at the sharp, splintered end. Without another thought, I stabbed it, hard, into the thigh of the man holding my arms. He screamed in pain and grabbed his leg. I left the mop handle in the man's leg.

Immediately after he let go, I turned to a shocked Not-Samar, "I'm going. Don't try to stop me," I said.

Not-Samar backed away, hands raised in surrender. I nodded, and then ran.

I recognised the streets I was running along, but I didn't recognise any of the sights. The buses were being driven by people, not an auto-driver. No autocops were to be seen. I could see a couple of people standing in the corner dressed in black with yellow reflective vests. One had his back to me and I could see the word 'police' on his yellow vest.

I ran over and they looked at me with concern.

"Hey, hang on. Stand back, you've got no mask on," said one of them.

"Oh, sorry," I said and I patted my pockets looking for one. "I think I forgot it. Can you help me? I'm a little lost," I said.

"Sure," said the other police officer, "where are you going?" He eyes me with more than a little suspicion.

"I'm trying to get home. Brixton House. But I've lost my way," I said.

Brixton House was the name of my old family building. The one where I thought Samar lived.

"I'm not familiar with that one," said the first guy. "One sec, I'll look it up." He then pulled out a small tablet-like device that I didn't recognise and started to type. His colleague was looking at me intently.

It was then I realised I was dressed in what could only be described as a jogging suit. Not something I'd usually wear, but these guys would not know. I felt out of place in my white suit.

As I stood there I heard the radios of the police officers squawk and then a voice, "Control to all units. Breakout at TTT. Escaped patient. Considered dangerous."

"Received, Control," said the officer looking at me, while never taking his eyes off me.

CHaPTer 11

This couldn't be real. Only a few hours ago I was sat in Samar's apartment, eating pizza and drinking beer.

Now Samar, or rather Not-Samar, was chasing me, wanting to lock me up and I was running away. Add that to the bizarre situation where I was staring down someone in an ancient police officer's uniform. They, in turn, were looking at me as though I were a dangerous person.

"Sir, can you tell me your name?" said the police officer to my right. This one had not been on his tablet device, and was teaching for something on his hip, attached to his belt.

"My name?" I asked.

"A simple question," the other officer, to my left added. He'd put away his device and he too was reaching for something attached to his belt.

"My name is," I hesitated when I noticed the one to my left was looking behind me.

I looked behind me in time to see a fist heading for my face. Then there was darkness.

"... But in the end Charles, all these changing laws, or as you like to call them 'rights infringements', they are going to improve your life and mine. Make them safer," said a voice in my deep subconscious.

"Are they? Are they really?" came the reply. There was a laugh; all deep in my sleepy subconscious.

I woke in my own bed. I was still dressed in my work clothes. My laptop, at the side of my bed, was playing a podcast on conspiracy theories. I fumbled for the space bar to pause the podcast. The screen showed me it was one of Samar's favourites, 'Mythbuster', also known as 'Charles Truth-Seeker' and 'Charlie Hates Lies'. He often talks a lot of crap, but the podcasts are usually very funny to listen to. He often took on local officials in his podcast, and always ripped them apart.

The podcast continued whilst I struggled in my sleepy haze to find the off-button for the crazy talk. Eventually I found the laptop lid and closed that instead. A second later and Charlie Hates Lies was silenced.

I sat up and rubbed my eyes. A crunchy squeak told me I needed to drink more. Either that or my eyes had been polished while I slept. The silence in the darkness of my room allowed me to think and to remember.

Memories of eating in Samar's apartment came to mind. A lovely evening with a life-long friend. Speaking to my mother, and realising there had been some horrible lies said to me and on my behalf. Finally, memories of Samar claiming he was not my friend and wanting me to be strapped to a gurney. The wrenching, churning sensation in the pit of my stomach told me that even my life-long friend had lied to me my whole life

Rising to my feet I found myself in the bathroom. My sleepy fog hid the memory of how I got here. I looked at my face in the mirror, rubbing my chin, and saw I needed a shave, badly. I must have neglected to shave for nearly a week to have this amount of growth. Usually, I struggled to grow decent facial hair and now I looked like an escapee.

Thoughts of escaping reminded me of the man I stabbed with the broken mop handle.

I scrunched my eyes shut and shook my head to clear away the thoughts.

When I opened my eyes again, I was staring at the rain outside my building. It was torrential rain, and I did not not want to go outside. My raincoat was on, I had my bag, I was ready for work. Still, I was hesitant. I knew that in this type of rain I would not be able to stay outside for long.

A vaguely familiar old man was coming from the rain, He shook off his hat and started to undo his coat. Holding the door, he stared at me over his rebreather. "Well? Are you going outside or not?" he asked.

His voice sounded far off and I had to shake my head to clear my thoughts. The old man shrugged, thinking I was not going outside, but then I stepped towards the door.

"Make up your mind," I heard him grumble under his breath as I passed him. He shrugged and moved towards the elevator, letting go of the door. I rushed for the door and pulled it open.

Outside the rain had stopped, and the ground all around me was dry. It had not rained for a while. My mind was racing. I realised that this could not be real. I was moving between things without knowing how I got there. Now that I was stood on the street, without a raincoat, without there being any rain, but a moment ago I was stood inside looking at the pouring rain.

I looked up and saw only a few clouds in the sky. I also saw an airplane. It was old fashioned compared to what I was used to seeing, this looked like it was easily two centuries old. It was thousands of feet above me, but even so I could see here were no sleek lines. The wings were almost at right-angles to the fuselage. It looked like it could carry passengers, but I could not tell from here if that was the case.

Was I slipping between time zones? Or was it dreams versus real life? This had to be a dream. In fact, was it all a dream? Am I about to wake up and see that I had fallen asleep in Samar's living room watching a dodgy holo about time travel?

A pain in my neck was beginning to develop and I was subconsciously rubbing where the pain was most serious. My hand came away wet. I looked at my hand and saw blood covering my fingers. Instinctively I reached around again and found an open wound just behind my left ear.

The light around me began to dim, and I realised I was sat in a room. Before me was a table. It was solid metal, as was the chair I sat on. The buzzing of the fluorescent bulb above my head was annoying the headache that was brewing in my temple.

This room has two doors, one to my left and the other to my right. Through the left door walked Not-Samar and through the right door walked my mother. They both took a chair each that I had not spotted were on the other side of the table.

"What is going on?" I said.

"Gordy," said my mother, "we are glad you are safe."

"Who are you people?" I asked. Frustration was beginning to build now too.

"We are here to look after you," said Not-Samar.

"You are not well," said my mother.

"I'm not well? I'll tell you this, you are all wrong. I am well, you are holding me against my will," I said.

"We are not holding you against your will. Here, look, this is your signature," said Not-Samar.

I looked a the document that Not-Samar thrust before me. It did have a signature on it, it was my name, it was not quite right. I stared at the paper for a moment, and then the signature changed to something more like my usual. However, the words of the statement made no sense to me. I could not read them at all. It was like the bang to my head was causing my brain to malfuction; I reached for the cut behind my ear. Blood was caked now and matted into my hair. Free flowing blood had stopped, that in itself made me feel better. The headache was still there, but I was feeling better in myself.

I picked up the sheet and tore it down the middle.

"Gordon!" said my mother.

"It is meaningless. There are no real words on this, no agreement from me," I said.

I flipped the table too. My mother and Not-Samar were startled and both of them jumped back, knocking over their chairs.

In the confusion I ran for the door to my left and pulled it open. The bright light outside the room made me squint, and I raised my free hand to cover my eyes. Dazed, I felt a shaking, rolling sensation.

"Gord, wake up man," said a familiar voice.

"I am awake," I said.

"You've cut your ear on your beer bottle," said the voice again.

I opened my eyes again and saw Samar looking at me with concern. He was holding a towel, offering it to me.

Looking around, I was in Samar's apartment. The blinds had been raised and the morning light was streaming through. The window had water running down the outside, obviously it was raining outside, but it wasn't heavy.

CHaPTer 12

"What is going on?" I said. I stumbled to my feet as I backed away, snatching the offered towel from Samar. In his other hand was broken pieces of beer bottle.

"Dude? It's me. Samar," he said.

"I don't know who you are anymore. What the hell have you done to me?" I said. Immediately I realised I was talking fast, I was scared, and I couldn't remember where I was for a moment.

"Nothing!" said Samar. He looked genuinely hurt by my accusation.

I pressed the towel to my head while I tried to hide my embarrassment. After a moment I looked at the towel to see how bad the damage was. A small amount of blood was soaked into the towel, the cut was thankfully not as bad as I thought it would be. However, the pain in my head was intense.

"No idea how you did it, man but you fell asleep on your bottle and it cracked, broke and you were cut by the pieces," said Samar.

I looked down at the chair and floor around. There was blood on the floor, and on shards of green glass scattered about. With my free hand I felt around my ear and the back of my head. Thankfully I could find no more cuts.

"I, I'm sorry," I said. "I must have been dreaming. What about I could not tell you. It was weird. More of a nightmare really."

Some images were bright and vivid in my mind, seeing my mother again, going to the museum, Not-Samar laughing. Others though were fading like a bad dream should. Still clutching the towel to my ear, I went to the bathroom to clean up.

"Hey, I've got to log on soon, but I'll make us some coffee," said Samar through the bathroom door.

"Okay," I said. The water from the tap started to wash the blood out of the towel. Steam billowed as fast flowing water heated up; my mind started to wander as images from the last day and my nightmare started to come back.

I left the tap running and stared into the mirror over the sink. The steam slowly started to fog the mirror while I studied my face. It was not a face I recognised any longer. I looked so tired, stubble shadowed my chin, and my hair was a mess. The deep bags under my eyes said I needed more sleep. As did the dark rings around my eyes.

With there being no window in here, the only light was the fluorescent tube above my head. The buzzing from the light caught my attention and I looked at that through the mirror instead, I couldn't look at myself any longer.

The light flickered and the room reflected in the mirror had changed. Instead of the powder blue painted walls, as were in most rooms of Samar's apartment, they were now a brilliant white. To my right, next to the sink, was an open, frosted-glass window. Outside the window I heard birds chirping. It sounded like there was no rain too.

I looked back at the mirror, almost fully fogged up by now. I swiped my hand over the glass to clear some of the fogging and the light flickered again.

I was back in the blue-walled bathroom of Samar's apartment. The towel in the sink had clogged up the drain and water was starting to spill over the top. The hot water burned my thumb as I held onto the sink.

Quickly, I pulled the towel aside and turned off the tap. Water gurgled down the drain. I found a dry towel and cleaned up the water from the floor. In the cabinet under the sink I found some gauze, tape, and some scissors. Using these, I taped up the cut on my ear.

Pinching my nose, I tried to push down another headache. The buzz of the light was not helping that endeavour.

It was time to go home and find out what the autocops had found about my apartment and the break-in. I ran my hand through my hair to straighten it out, adding some water to help with the process. It wasn't a good look, but it would do.

"Hey Samar, I think I'm going to go home," I said as I opened the bathroom door.

The view outside the room was wrong. Again the walls were a brilliant white. It wasn't Samar's apartment, this was the museum. I closed and opened the door, to check I want going mad. The walls were not blue, or white. Instead, it was now my childhood home, which was three doors down from Samar's in this building. Again a shot of pain hit my temple from this headache, making me shake my head.

When I opened my eyes Samar was stood before me holding a cup of coffee for me. It smelled great. Thankfully, I was back in Samar's apartment again. The look on my face obviously caused concern in my friend.

"What up?" asked Samar.

"Nothing," I lied. "Trying to clear this headache. Had it for a while now."

"Drink up, you look like you need a shot of 'wake-me-up'. This'll get you going. Might not help you head though." He then passed me the cup.

"Yeah. Probably." I took a big gulp of the hot brew. It was nearly too hot, but I didn't spit it back out.

The coffee was like a jolt of electricity to my brain. The headache wasn't helped, as predicted, but at least I was awake now.

"Got to see how my apartment looks," I said.

"You heard from the autocops?"

"Not yet, but I'll call them on my way over. If I can't get in I'm on the way to work too, I'll just get the next bus if I can't go home yet."

"You're going to work looking like that?" he scoffed. "You'll scare the pants off everyone. You look homeless. You don't want to get mistaken for a 'burned', do you?"

I shook my head. That was a mistake. Pain burst into colours before my eyes. Images of Dead Guy resurfaced, and I had to grip the door frame to stop me from collapsing.

"And," he continued, "you look like you need something for your head."

"I'll be fine. Let me get outside and maybe fresh air will help clear these cobwebs," I gently tapped my head when I spoke.

Samar shrugged. "Cool. But here," he walked over to the door, grabbed his coat, and came back to me. "It's raining hard out there so you'll need the extra protection."

The coat looked like a top of the line one and looked like it cost a lot of money.

I looked at Samar and was about to question where he got it from, when he spoke again.

"Yes, it is expensive. However, it will keep you dry for quite a while," he said.

"Thanks, I'll get it back to you," I said.

"I know where you live," he smiled.

I put the coat on and went into the living room to get my bag. Samar's computer was chiming. "Someone is calling you," I said.

"Ah, crap! The meeting started ten minutes ago. Gotta get into it. Call me later," he said as he ran to his chair.

I smiled and watched him scramble about, sitting down, waking his computer up, and logging into the call. The frantic pace was immediately replaced by a cool and calm demeanor as he answered the call.

With my bag slung over my shoulder, I headed to the door.

CHAPTER 13

I made my way out onto the street outside Samar's building. The rain was considerable, but Samar's coat was amazing. Not only was it stylish, but I was warm and dry almost all the way to my feet. It was a long coat, longer than something I would ever choose. The quality and comfort off this coat made me feel like taking a walk instead of going home. However, walks were not really practical these days thanks to the constant rain.

It was only a short walk over to my apartment building, so I pulled up the hood and set off. There was very little traffic on the road, which was slightly unusual for this time of day. It made me think that there was a bad storm coming. Usually, people stayed home more whenever the forecast was for extreme rain. I'd not seen any weather forecast recently, I tended to stay away from such things. It was normally depressing.

The dreams I'd had, for that's all they could be, were no more than flashes now, but I tried to focus on them. I didn't want to forget what happened, even though I now knew they were not real.

Thoughts of my recent conversation with Samar popped into my head and reminded me that I needed to call about my apartment. From my bag I took out my tablet while also looking for some respite from the rain. A nearby bus shelter proved to be the perfect place. I dialled the number for the autocops.

The call was answered almost immediately, "Citizen Twist. Thank you for calling. Your call is appreciated. You should have called before now, it is important you stay where you are. Your safety is important."

"My safety? What do you mean?" I said.

I started to think of Dead Guy, and his note. The note had read 'our safety is of utmost importance to us', the words were fixed in my head. My hand went straight to my pocket, where I found the crumpled ball of paper. The seat behind me in the bus shelter caught me as I staggered backwards. I pulled out the ball of paper and held it in my hand as I confined to talk to the autocop.

My mind was reeling and I started to doubt what was real, and dream again. on two occasions now, someone or something was trying to make sure I was safe. But why?

"Citizen Twist, please reveal your location," said the autocop on screen.

"What did you find in my apartment?" I asked. Other questions were vying for attention, but I wanted to avoid them for now.

"There were some fingerprints found of the gentleman who you saw expire before you last week," it said.

"You mean yesterday, don't you?" I said. It could not have been more than that, it had to have been yesterday. Where had four days gone? I recalled going round to Samar's only last night and he ordered beer and pizzas. I was not there for more than a night.

"No, Citizen Twist. The altercation with the deceased was four days ago. You have been missing since then," was the reply.

"Four days? Missing? That's not right," I was shouting, and people around me were looking at me with concern.

"Please. Your safety is a priority. Please reveal your location."

"I am on my way to work," I lied, and then I ended the call.

With my tablet back in my bag once more, I started to jog, then sprint, towards home. I needed to get there before the autocops, and leave before they arrive.

As I raced along the streets, people jumped out of my way. The rain splattered the parts of my face above my rebreather, each raindrop stung. I tried pulling the hood of my coat further out, and I dropped my chin as I ran to stop as much or the painful rain as I could.

My building was just across the street, but I had to stop. I saw two autocops walking towards the front door. I ducked into a doorway, out of view and watched. They walked straight pass the door and continued down the street. I don't think they saw me, or even if they were aware of my conversation a moment ago.

While I waited a moment, I unravelled the balled up note in my hand. Reading it again, the words still did not make sense. Why me? Why am I important?

When the autocops were finally out of sight, I ran over and entered. The lobby was empty, which made me feel I was probably ahead of the autocops trying to see me right now.

The elevator seemed to be taking longer than usual, and I was willing it to move faster. When the doors finally opened, out stepped an old man. I recognised him immediately, despite the change of rebreather. This was maybe the third time I had seen him, and in two different apartment buildings.

"Hey, it's you. I've seen you before! More than once. Haven't I?" I said.

The old man's face, what I could see over his mask, blanched. It was then I realised I'd taken off my rebreather and I was standing quite close to the man. Intimidatingly close.

"I don't know what you mean," said the old man. He pressed himself up against the opposite wall as he tried to exit the lobby, trying to keep as much distance from me as he could.

"No. I do know you! Who the hell are you? Why do we keep meeting?" I was stepping towards him as he tried to escape from me. Anger and confusion were all I could feel right now.

The old man reached the front door and frantically pulled it open. Before I could speak again, he'd bolted. He was quite spritely for an old man. I didn't have time to give chase, there were more important things to do.

Hearing the doors of the elevator starting to close, a familiar metallic scrape I'd heard a thousand times before, brought me back to the task at hand. I jumped back to the elevator and stuck my hand into the gap just in time. The sensors realised, the doors responded and I was allowed to enter.

I tapped my foot impatiently as the elevator rode up to the twenty third floor. When the doors opened again, the site before me was unfamiliar. Again, the world had changed. The carpets were clean, that had never been the case as long as I had lived here.

The doors to all the apartments were all a different style to what I had seen for the last nine years. I was used to a dark, muddy brown and the apartment numbers had always been a dull brass.

Now though, all the walls and the doors were bright white, and the door numbers were black. The numbers could have been painted metal, but they looked plastic. Fluorescent tubes buzzed over my head. Also, none of the doors had a keypad entry.

I sprinted to my door, which again I could see was already open. A little déjà vu was lurking in the back of my mind. Inside I could hear someone walking about.

"Hello?" I shouted through the opening. Memories of my trashed apartment surfaced.

A glass, or a plate, smashed and I could hear whispered cursing.

"I can hear you," I said. All movement inside stopped. "I'm coming in."

I pushed the door wider, and the occupant rushed through. The black-clad figure knocked me over as they passed. I banged my head on the floor as I fell, but I managed to catch a glimpse of the intruder.

It was clearly a man, but his features were hidden behind a rebreather. He ran through the door to the stairs, he didn't wait for the elevator.

When I stood, confusion was again replaced with familiarity. The doors were back to the horrible dark brown with brass numbers. The door to my apartment was firmly closed, and the keypad screen showed it had last been locked up by the autocops.

I rubbed my head and tried to ignore the odd flashes. Pain pinged across my forehead, another headache was brewing. Or was it the same one?

The keypad on my door was waiting so I entered my PIN code, the door beeped, there was a snick, and my door opened.

I wanted two things from home; clean clothes and shower. I believed I only had time to change though.

Whilst I changed I looked about to see what, if anything, the autocops had done during their investigation. Nothing had been tidied up, I hadn't expected that, but thought they may have picked up the two fallen chairs. I replaced seat covers, cushions, and some ornaments on a side table one of my mother's prized ceramic figurines, an angel holding a baby, was broken. The head had snapped clean off.

I took it to the kitchen to look for some glue. As I walked, I could feel something inside the body of the angel rattling about. Looking within, I could see what looked like a memory stick. Without another thought I hit the angel against the kitchen counter.

In the midst of the broken white pieces, the black memory stick stood out. I removed the cap from one end to see a standard USB connector, and I could see it would go into my tablet easily.

There was a knock at the door, "Citizen Twist, this is officer Z9@West, please open the door."

"Please wait," I said.

"Citizen Twist, please open the door." It sounded insistent.

I had to think fast. Firstly, I had to see what was on this memory stick. Secondly, I had to leave.

"Please prove you're an autocop," I said. i knew it was, no one used the title of 'citizen' other than the autocops.

I was stalling, the autocop would sense that soon enough and probably try to force entry. With the memory stick in my hand, I grabbed my tablet and plugged it in.

Almost immediately there was a screeching sound. It was painful to hear and I was forced to plug one ear with a finger, but my other hand I was hampered. Holding the tablet I could only cover my other ear with the heel of my hand.

The noise only lasted around ten seconds. It ended with a thud outside of my door. I opened the door and saw the autocop face down. Its operator ID was blank. Nudging it with my foot resulted in no response.

I took that as a hint, ran back inside and grabbed my bag, Samar's coat and my tablet, and made a break for it.

Chapter 14

I didn't wait for the elevator. It would take too long. Running down the stairs would certainly be easier. And much faster. It definitely would confuse any autocops that may be waiting on the ground floor. I may even be able to slip out of the back door if they were waiting for me by the elevator.

By the time I reached the fifteenth floor, I started to get breathless. So much so that I had to stop at the fourteenth or I was going to fall down the rest of these stairs. Stopping on the landing I gulped in the air. There were dots and stars in my vision; I was not fit enough to be doing this.

In between breaths I heard the echo of a door somewhere below me open and then close. This was followed by the echoes of a tell-tale electronic chattering whir. That told me an autocop had entered the stair well, and it was communicating with base, or possibly a partner. It might be concerned on why it was not getting a reply. They sometimes worked in pairs.

Immediately I pressed myself against the wall, away from the railings of the stairs. I needed a different plan.

The door to the fourteenth floor looked inviting, and the only sensible route to take right now. Opening it cautiously, I peered down the corridor both ways. No autocops. I went through and looked for the janitor's cupboard; each floor had them. It was straight across from me.

They were never locked. Who of the residents would need what was inside? A ratty old mop and a rusting bucket were all that was in here, aside from dust and a disturbing number of cobwebs.

It was small, but large enough to let me sit down on the floor and fully close the door. There was no light in here, but that was fine. My tablet would give me enough light.

Once I had settled down, I picked up my tablet and again plugged in the memory stick. There was no sound this time, thankfully. With no ear piercing sound being triggered, I was able to have a look at what files were stored on the stick.

I navigated to the file system and found two folders and a single file. The file, called 'Alarm', was an app, and I could see it was already running. Guessing this was the thing that caused the screech earlier, I stopped the app. I didn't want the autocops, or anyone else, to know where I was by it going off again.

I couldn't tell why the app had started earlier but not this time. I guess it must automatically be triggered to start if the memory stick is plugged into a device and an automaton, such as an autocop, was detected nearby. Fortunately, none were obviously near enough now or the alarm would be sounding at the moment. It was nice to know if I wanted to evade the autocops in the near future.

With a little reprieve from 'the chase', I looked at the two folders. One was labelled 'Docs', and the other was 'Vid'. Not being much into reading, I looked at 'Vid' first.

Inside the folder was a single video file called 'Gordon'. Immediately my interest was piqued, but I had to be careful. Assuming the video would have sound as well as visuals, I looked in my pockets for some earphones. I found an old wired set, only the left earpiece properly worked, but it would do.

With the earphones in place, I started the video. The right earpiece crackled, so I removed it from my ear. The sound was annoying.

The image on the video was flipped ninety degrees left, and it looked like the camera was pointed at the ceiling. In the background I could hear someone talking, but not clearly enough to be understood. As the video continued, the audio cleaned up.

"No, put that down. Put it down! Silly dog," said my mother. It was definitely her voice. There was another, a man, "Good. Thank you. Who's a good boy?"

My mother's voice went quiet as she moved away from the mic, then it became clear again.

"Sit!" she said, and then she was visible on screen. "Oh, the image is wrong. One sec," she reached forward and the whole image was replaced with her palm. The image then went dark as her hand covered the lens.

There was a clatter, and then her hand was moved away. Now the image was in landscape format, and I could see her face clearly. She smiled, took a deep breath, and then began to speak.

"Gordon, what you know is a lie. Now don't worry, it's not all bad, but you do need to do something," she sighed and wiped her brow. I could see concern line her face.

"You're stuck, but we have a plan. Your Dad and me," she said.

Why was she talking about my Dad as if he is still alive? I checked the date of the file, but what I saw made no sense. The file properties were all set as if it had been created in nineteen forty five, at midnight on the first of January. That could not be right, this must have been deliberately set to these values, or the computer it was created on had not been configured correctly. The other files were similarly dated.

I'd not been paying attention to the video while looking at the files, so I tracked back the position marker to where she mentioned my Dad.

"We are very worried about you, son," said my Dad as he came into frame. He was holding a small dog in his arms, which was trying desperately to get out of his grip. The dog's tail was wagging, and it looked happy. It had probably been playing with my Dad before he came onto the video.

"Ow! Bingo!" said my Dad as Bingo had nipped at his fingers. He put the dog down.

Both my Mother and my Dad were alive, and I was now more confused than ever.

"Peter, take the dog outside," said my Mother. "I'm talking to Gordon."

I heard my Dad grumble something, and then he was gone.

"Gordon, you need to find the exit. I know what that sounds like, but that's the only clue I have for you. No one here can do any more for you. The machines are keeping you alive, but we can't remove the headset without hurting you."

"The doctor here said that you need to look for a white room. That's where the exit is," she said.

The memories of the white room came flooding back. The Not-Samar, the man I stabbed with a broken broom, the strangely dressed police. All of it.

"You've been there before, but you fought the game characters. We saw it all on the screen in the arena," she said.

"When you go back, you need to avoid the game characters as much as possible. The AI of the game will have put something in to make them want revenge. I don't understand it all, you're the technical one of the family, but that's is what the people here are telling me."

I paused the video. "This is making no sense," I said out loud. Immediately I regretted speaking especially as I heard the floorboards outside creak.

I stopped breathing, hoping I hadn't been heard. Seconds felt like hours as I held my breath. A shadow of someone stepping up the the janitor's cupboard door appeared.

Two shapes under the foot of the door, looking like feet or legs, were visible, and then a familiar voice.

"I'm sorry, officer, I've not seen Mr. Twist," said the building manager, Hech.

I heard his hand on the door handle, but as he started to turn the handle I also heard his tablet chiming. Someone was calling him. He let go off the door handle and started to talk on the call.

His voice trailed off as he wandered away from the cupboard. I let out a long breath.

I waited a few moments and listened at the door. There were no sound coming from the other side. It was completely silent.

A moment longer and I decided to risk it. I cracked the door open a touch. There was no-one in my eye line. I stepped out, listening and looking as much as possible. I quietly closed the door and headed for the stairs again.

Around the corner of the corridor I could hear the autocop. Time to really get out of here.

I ran down the stairs to the ground floor. It was an arduous task, as was the run from twenty three to fourteen. Breathless, I pushed open the door the lobby. No autocops. That was a relief.

I pulled my coat tight, put my rebreather on, pulled up the hood and left.

Outside, the rain was extreme. That storm I'd predicted earlier had hit hard. I would not be able to stay out very long in this.

Across the street I saw an autotaxi dropping off a fare. I ran over and tapped on the glass of the driver's window.

The automated driver turned to look at me. "Can I be of assistance?" it said.

"Can you take me to the Museum Of Technology?" I said.

"It is against protocol," said the driver.

"I'll pay double," I said.

The driver hesitated. It's head twitched from side to side.

"Okay, triple! That's all I can afford, I said. The rain was pelting me hard; I needed this driver to bite.

It was unusual to barter with a taxi driver. Their programming would not usually permit this level of conversation, but this one was wavering.

I stepped closer to hopefully hide my face from onlookers. Outside my building I saw two autocops exit, they were obviously conversing in their electronic chatter. Working out what to do next.

"Well?" I said.

"One moment please," said the driver.

If it's eyes were human, they would have glazed over. It was contacting the autotaxi head office for advice. A moment later and it turned back to me.

"That is acceptable. Please deposit your payment here," it said as a panel near to the side mirror moved inwards and thumb pad payment sensor appeared from within.

I saw the price and nearly changed my mind. It was a lot of money for such a short journey.

With my thumb on the device, I watched as the reader light bobbed up and down the sensor plate.

Eventually there was a ding as my payment was accepted. With a heavy heart, having spent far too much money, I stepped inside and sat down.

Almost immediately the autotaxi started to move off.

"It is awful weather we are having today, is it not?" said the driver. This one had been installed with a small talk subroutine.

"Yes," I said. I wasn't interested in chatting. "How long before we get there?"

"A mere moment, sir," it replied.

EPILOGUE

Whilst I sat there in the autotaxi, I picked up my tablet again and resumed the video. With the earpiece still in my left ear, the driver could not hear anything.

"Please get to the museum again, you can then get home. We are all missing you," said my mother.

The video ended there. A still image of my smiling mother reaching for the stop button on the video recording software. I brushed my fingers over the image and smiled too. "I'm coming," I said.

"I am sorry, sir. Did you say something?" said the driver.

"No, sorry. Was thinking out loud. Just ignore me," I said.

"As you wish sir," it said.

We carried on in silence. The ten minute drive to the museum was long enough for me to look at the files in the 'Docs' folder on the memory stick. There were three files. One was the picture that Samar showed me, which I found highly suspicious. How did Samar find this same image when he did his searching? It was highly coincidental.

In fact, there was a bigger question that needed to be answered. It was extremely convenient that this memory stick just happened to be in the broken angel. Extremely convenient that is was placed somewhere that I would find. On top of all that, it was extremely convenient that the video from my mother was there too, and that she mentioned my previous trip to the museum. If this was a game, as my mother says, then how did they know I would find the memory stick?

Pieces of this puzzle were still needed, and then I needed to put them all together. Hopefully, answers were in the museum.

Another file in the 'Docs' folder was a letter from a Doctor Henry Sefton, all about me being trapped in my own game world. Allegedly, I was connected to a VR system, which included a suit and a headset. They had tried to get me out of the suit, on several occasions, but each time I had fought back with my actions in the game world, or actions that happened to me in the game world.

The last item in the 'Docs' folder appeared to be a scanned file, this was called 'Dr. Sefton ID Scan'. I opened it and saw it was a document with a scanned image of the ID badge of this Dr Sefton. Worryingly, the image of the man was familiar.

I zoomed in to the image and then it hit me. The eyes, they were those of the old man I kept on seeing!

Now I knew the name of the old man, but what is his connection to all this.

"Here we are," said the driver.

I hadn't realised, but the autotaxi had stopped and sure enough I could see the museum. It dominated this street, it was the largest building I had ever seen aside from apartment blocks. The twenty pillars that lined the front of the building, separated by the front door, were the most striking feature of the building.

"Thank you," I said to the driver.

The doors unlocked and I got out. A chill wind blew the rain at my face making me pull up the hood of my coat. The street light above my head buzzed, flickered on, then off, and then came back on. The darkness created by the storm triggered the light to come on.

It wasn't late in the day, but the storm clouds made it dark enough to feel like early evening. The comments from the autocop about me being missing for days, and the deceptive light conditions were giving me concerns. Was time passing at the right speed? Was I really stuck inside some kind of simulation?

I shook my head to clear my thoughts, the headache I'd been nursing for a while struck behind my eyes again. Flashes of light strobed across my vision.

I waited for the pain, the lights and the dizziness to subside before I took another step. Holding on to the lamp post helped me stay on my feet.

When the haze in my head cleared I set off for the front door. The large black, double doors were closed. It was mid-afternoon, the doors should be open. As far as I remember the museum usually opened nine till nine. There was no way it was already after nine right now. I tried the doors and found they were locked.

I had to get inside, there must be a way in. The side door I exited by last time would possibly be the way I needed to go in. I walked down the street trying to find another door.

After walking for a while, following the outline of the building, I hadn't found a door. Eventually I did find the rear entrance, where delivery vehicles would bring new exhibits for the museum.

The gates were open, I could see a vehicle parked up near a service door. Light spilled from within and I spied my chance.

I looked around, but I couldn't see anyone. I had to make a break for it before I was stopped by security or any other staff.

Staying behind bins and outbuildings, and in the shadows as much as I could, I quietly made my way over to the door. No sound could be heard, so I ran inside.

There was was a large warehouse here. Boxes and crates were everywhere, but no people. I started to think this was too easy.

"You!" shouted a voice behind me.

I froze. The voice was instantly recognisable. I slowly turned to see Not-Samar standing there. Anger fuelled his features.

The words of my mother rang in my head, 'interact with the characters in the game as little as possible.' I immediately ran away.

"You can't hide," he said.

"I don't need to hide," I shot back. I didn't stop running, there had to be an entrance into the museum from here.

Behind me I heard Not-Samar start taking on a radio, "Alexei, get to the warehouse. Our friends is back," he said.

There was an electronic squelch, and then a reply. "Yeah? I'll get the broken broom handle ready. I'd love me some payback."

Alexei must be the one I attacked last time I was here. I was glad he was okay, aside from the injury I'd caused, but at the same time I hoped the wounds I'd caused meant he was too slow and I could evade him.

I found two black doors, above them the sign read 'Offices'. The white room must be this way.

The doors both had a 'Pull' sign on them, and I obliged. I pulled both doors. They swung easily, they were much lighter than I had expected.

As I was stepping through the doors I could see the hulking brute I'd stabbed with the broken broom. He was hobbling badly from the far end of the corridor. The doors were in the middle, meaning I could run the other way.

"Come here," shouted Alexei.

There was no chance of me staying around, nor was there any real chance of being caught either.

Ahead the corridor turned left. I had no choice, either turn back or turn left. Going back was suicide. Left it had to be. I had to find the white room again.

I was playing the words of my mother in my head again, 'the white room is where the exit is'. The irony was not lost on me. This white room felt like it was in the centre of this large building, and that was where the exit was meant to be found.

As I ran down these long, echoing corridors, I tried to remember what the corridor outside the white room looked like. The floors had grey carpets, and the doors had no markings.

There was a set of double doors ten feet ahead, through them came the woman who had tried to strap me onto the gurney. An evil gain on her face.

"There is no where for you to go," she said.

Instead of stopping I just picked up speed. My lungs were burning with all the running, but I charged into her. Her slight frame was no obstacle, I bowled her over into the doors. We tumbled over and over, with me ending up in the dominant position.

"Where is the white room?" I asked. I had her pinned to the floor with my hands gripping the lapels of her lab coat.

Unfortunately, I wasn't paying attention to where her hand was. In her right hand she held a baton, which she whacked into my temple.

Everything I knew was replaced with pain. She had not unseated me, but she was not done trying. I raised my hand to defend another strike, the baton rang against my forearm.

With my other arm, I punched her in the face. I hated doing it; I've never hit anyone in anger before. I didn't like what this nightmare was turning me into.

The woman was unconscious. I tested for her pulse to make sure I'd only knocked her out. Thankfully I found a pulse on her neck. The mark on her face where I'd punched was already swelling. She'd feel that for a while.

I stood and went the way I thought she had come from. There was only one way possible to go.

Through another set of double doors, these were white. I must be near. The corridor beyond was familiar.

There was grey carpets on the floor, and all the doors were white with no markings. I noticed a dark patch on the floor, that must be the blood stain from the man whose nose I kicked.

That must mean the door to my immediate left was the room in which I'd been held.

I stepped over to the door and took a deep breath, this was it. Hopefully an end to what had been happening to me.

I opened the door and stepped into the room. The long mirrored window along the opposite wall greeted me, as did both Samar, and Not-Samar.

"I knew you'd be coming here," said Not-Samar. I wanted to wipe the smug smile off his face.

Not-Samar was wearing a lab coat, a stark contrast to what Samar was wearing. Samar was wearing jeans and a tatty old t-shirt with a faded print of an old movie poster.

"Dude," said Samar, "where did you think you were going? I'm trying to help you."

I looked from one to the other, images of old cartoons came to mind. The old angel-on-one-shoulder-and-the-devil-on-the-other trope. Each one with a different demand of the protagonist.

"I just want to go home," I said.

"You are home," said Not-Samar.

"This is not a home!" I screamed. "This is a nightmare."

The speaker above the mirror crackled into life. "Gordon, this is the exit," said my mother.

"She doesn't know what she is saying," said Samar.

"I know what I want to say though, and that is this. Let me go," I said.

I was weary, and longed for a simpler time. One without old men dying in the street calling my name, one without being chased away from museums. A world where life made sense again.

The door behind me opened and Alexei came through. I moved away, into the centre of the room.

The only furniture in here was a single stool with the obligatory white seat. Everything white. The walls, door, carpet and ceiling were all white.

I moved towards the stool, which was near the mirror. Everyone moved around the room to maintain their space from my position.

"What is behind this mirror?" I said. I jerked my head behind to point to the mirror.

Immediately Not-Samar and Samar both looked anxious.

"It's just a mirror," stammered Samar.

"Why would there be anything behind the mirror?" said Not-Samar.

"Let's see shall we?" I said. I picked up the stool and threw it at the mirror.

Time slowed.

There was only one door in this room, but this was apparently the exit. It made sense to me that the only way out was to go through the mirror.

I watched everything in slow motion. The stool flew majestically through the air. Both Samar and Alexei covered their faces. Not-Samar was mouthing the word 'no' in an exaggerated way.

The stool went through the mirror.

Glass shards flew in all directions.

I felt the earth beneath my feet turn.

Behind the mirror was only darkness. No light, no people watching me. Nothing.

The room tilted, and I was pitched into the dark hole left by the mirror. I saw Samar, Not-Samar and Alexei disappear into the distance.

I was falling into nothing. I couldn't see anything in the deep dark, even my own hands.

"Gordon?" said my Dad. He was on my right in this brightly lit room.

The light hurt my eyes. I tried to squint to see even a little of the world about me. The light was too bright, I could not make anything out clearly.

"Oh my god! Gordon," said my mother. "Peter, get the doctors!"

A moment later an elderly man, judging by the voice spoke. "Mr. Twist I am Doctor Sefton, can you hear me? We have spoken before, but I'm still waiting for your replies."

I turned to where the voice was coming from, but I couldn't make it any details.

"That's good," said Sefton. I'd drifted out of the conversation. "Let me run a few quick tests."

I felt a hand on my face pull open my left eye, then my right, each time someone shone a bright light in my eye.

"Mrs. Twist," said Sefton. "It will still take some time. Not everyone recovers fully from these injuries."

"What's going on?" I was screaming at the room.

"He's still not well," continued Sefton, ignoring my question.

"But he's opened his eyes," said my Dad.

"I'm right here, Dad," I said. He didn't seem to hear me. "Dad?"

"I'm afraid that right now, I'm not sure he will recover. He's what some call 'locked in'. There's debate about how much someone in his condition understands, but we will continue to look after him," said Sefton.

"I'm right here. I'm not locked in," I said. "Can you hear me? Please say you can. Hello?"